The Way I am is Different

(A Children's Book about a boy with Fetal Alcohol Spectrum Disorder.)

By: Helen Simpson-Orcutt

Today I start Grade 3 and I am pretty nervous.

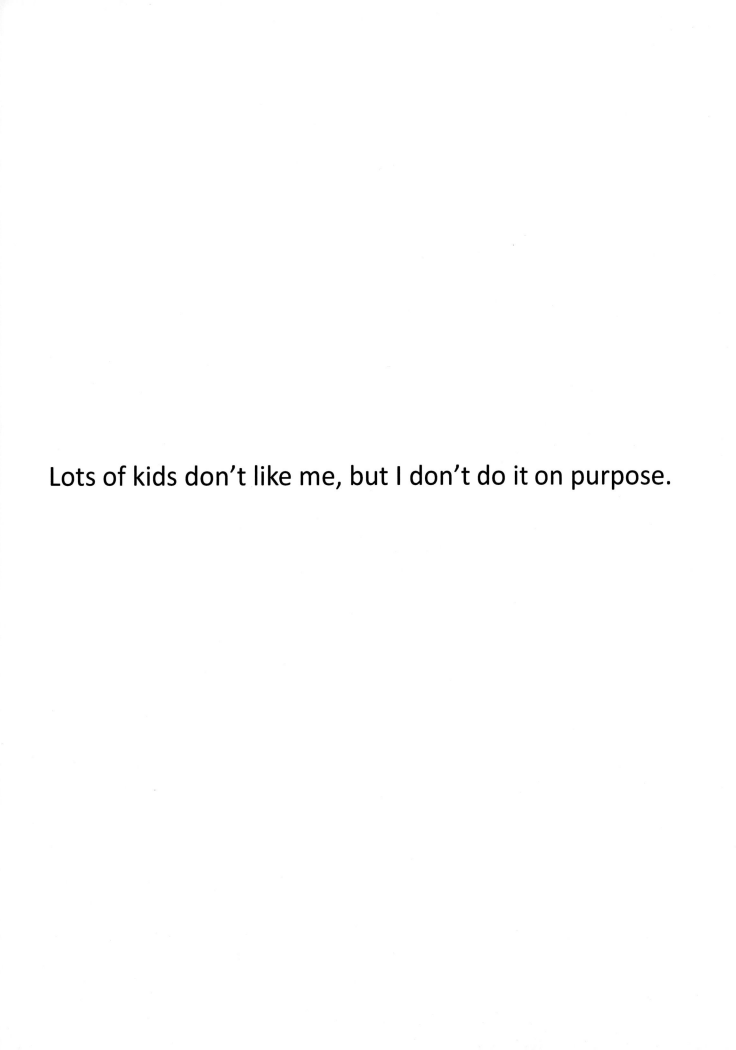

Lots of kids don't like me, but I don't do it on purpose.

My mom drank when I was in her belly, so learning for me is different.

When the teachers give instructions, I'll only get it if they repeat it.

Not once or twice, but probably 4 or 5 times more.

Please don't get frustrated teacher, I don't think you're a bore.

I'm trying to pay attention, but it's really, really hard.

I get overwhelmed easily, and act out and play a part.

My mom tells me I'm a good boy, and only when she says it do I believe it.

Then I get to school and no one else can see it.

I really like having friends but making them isn't easy.

They think that I am strange or tell me that I am crazy.

I am just a little boy who wants to be like everyone else I see.

I am just a little boy who doesn't like being me.

It's not my fault I'm different, it was not my choice.

Today I'm going to try and be brave, and find my voice.

It's okay that I learn different and it's okay I'm not the same.

It's okay that my senses feel different and its okay I can't feel pain.

It's okay it takes me longer to get dressed in the morning.

It's okay if I need a lot of hugs and if I need you to read me a story.

I've got a lot of days ahead of me and I got lots of stuff to do.

So every day I'll try and do better and I'll learn something new.

Mom, so please tell me I am a good boy each and every day.

Please remind me it's okay to be different and I will be okay.

The End.

If you ever get down or start to think you're not special, just remember there are people out there that think the absolute most of you. You sweet child, are very special and loved.